(4)

Margaret Ziegler Is Horse-Crazy

by Crescent Dragonwagon

illustrated by Peter Elwell

Macmillan Publishing Company   New York

BY THE SAME AUTHOR

Alligator Arrived with Apples
Always, Always
Dear Miss Moshki
Diana, Maybe
Half a Moon and One Whole Star
Jemima Remembers

Macmillan Publishing Company, 866 Third Avenue, New York, NY 10022
Collier Macmillan Canada, Inc.
First Edition   Printed in the United States of America

10 9 8 7 6 5 4 3 2 1

The text of this book is set in 13-point ITC Century Light.
The illustrations are rendered in pen-and-ink with wash.
Library of Congress Cataloging-in-Publication Data
Dragonwagon, Crescent. Margaret Ziegler is horse-crazy.
Summary: Margaret is crazy about horses until she finally gets a chance
to ride at Country Life Riding Day Camp. [1. Horses—Fiction]
I. Elwell, Peter, ill. II. Title.
PZ7.D7824Mar 1988   [Fic]   87-23975   ISBN 0-02-733230-6

For Marcia Yearsley,
who always gets back on
—C.D.

For Becky
—P.E.

argaret Ziegler is horse-crazy. That's what everybody says. Her mother says it. Her father says it. Her big brother, Rodney, who is always leaving to go to softball practice, says it.

"She's never even been *on* a horse!" says Rodney, snorting.

But Margaret knows better.

It is true she has never ridden on a horse. But soon she will, this summer, at Country Life Riding Day Camp.

Meanwhile, Margaret has a collection of twenty-three horses. Five are made of china, one is made of wood, and seventeen are made of plastic. All of them have names.

"This is Windy, and this is Sundowner, and this is Butterscotch, and this is Luna...."

Meanwhile, she can gallop like a horse. She can also canter, trot, whinny, and neigh, but only when Rodney isn't around. Rodney sniffs and shakes his head. "Not a horse," he says, "but, yeah, you're sure *some* kind of an animal!" He doesn't understand. No one does. They will, though ... after she begins to ride this summer at Country Life Riding Day Camp.

Meanwhile, Margaret draws horses. She makes a circle for the body above the front legs, and a circle for the body above the back legs, and a smaller circle and an oval for the head. Then she connects the circles, drawing in the neck and back and legs, drawing in a mane flying up and a tail flying out. All the pages of her notebook at school are covered with horses. When her class has Art, she paints a whole field of horses: a red horse, a blue horse, a green horse, a yellow horse, a purple horse.

"Purple horses!" says Rodney. "Boy, she's really gone off the deep end now!"

"Rodney, leave your sister alone," says their mother. "She's just at the age where she's a little horse-crazy."

Rodney shakes his head and asks if he can be excused. He leaves the table, rolling his eyes.

But Margaret doesn't care. When she begins to ride at Country Life Riding Day Camp, they'll see.

Meanwhile, Margaret has a poster of horses up in her room. She studies it.

When her parents' friends, the Sneeds, come to visit, she shows the poster to Mr. and Mrs. Sneed.

"These are the Percherons. They are the work horses," Margaret explains. "These are the Morgans. They are the kind of horse policemen ride. They are very intelligent and loyal."

"That's nice, dear," says Mrs. Sneed. "And now we really have to—"

"This is an Appaloosa," says Margaret. "And this is a pinto, and this is a palomino, and these little ones over here—they are the way horses looked in prehistoric times."

The Sneeds shift from foot to foot.

"Fred? Irene?" calls Margaret's mother.

"Margaret got you trapped up there with her horses?" calls Margaret's father. "C'mon down."

"Thank you for telling us about your horses," says Mrs. Sneed.

"You certainly know a lot about them," says Mr. Sneed.

The Sneeds go downstairs.

From upstairs, Margaret hears her father say, "She's just a little horse-crazy, is all."

She hears her mother say, "She's at that age."

But she'll show them, and soon.

Meanwhile, Margaret wins a prize at school for reading the most books of any child in the third grade. She has read 157 books in one year, all of them about horses. The librarian has had to borrow many of the books from other libraries. "Don't you think you should expand your horizons, dear?" the librarian asks her. In class, Margaret has done book reports on *Misty of Chincoteague, Black Beauty,* and *National Velvet.* But when she does *How to Groom Your First Horse,* her teacher says, "Margaret…it's important to be well-rounded."

Well-rounded, thinks Margaret, like a ball, like the stupid softball Rodney is always carrying and tossing and catching in his glove. Hah! thinks Margaret. They won't tell me that after they've seen me ride at Country Life Riding Day Camp.

Sometimes Margaret lies in bed at night, imagining she is grooming a horse. She picks up one foot, carefully cleaning out the dirt around the horseshoe with a hoof pick. Then she does the other three feet. Then she brushes the horse all over with a currycomb. She can almost feel how velvety the horse's smooth neck will be. She can almost feel how much the horse will like being groomed by her.

But mostly what she thinks about is what will happen at Country Life Riding Day Camp.

What will happen, Margaret knows, is this.

Her parents will let her out of the car, and she will walk to a paddock. A big black horse will be in the center of the paddock, rearing up on his back legs and whinnying loudly. "That's Midnight," someone will whisper to Margaret. "He went wild. No one can get near him."

Fearlessly, quickly, before anyone can stop her,
Margaret will slip into the pasture. When they see her,
everyone will gasp, "Get that child out of there! She
could get hurt!" But it will be too late.

"Here, Midnight," Margaret will call softly, and
Midnight will stop rearing. He will toss his head once and
trot gently over to Margaret, who will pat him on his
graceful black neck, on his velvety nose. "Good boy,"
Margaret will tell Midnight, as she catches his bridle and
leads him back toward the stable.

As she passes through the crowd she will hear people whisper, "She has a way with horses." And as she grasps Midnight and pulls herself up onto his back, as they ride away together, she will hear more whispers. "It's a miracle!" "That girl is a natural." "No one's been able to ride that horse for *years*." "She and Midnight are made for each other."

This is what Margaret *knows* will happen at Country Life Riding Day Camp.

But what really happens is this.

At Country Life Riding Day Camp there is a line of twenty-eight girls standing on a ramp waiting for their first riding lesson.

"Attention, please," calls a man holding a clipboard. "I am Mr. Duke. I will call your names and assign you each a horse for today. After I've called your name, stand over there, and Greta, my assistant, will bring your horse out to you. Just stand by your horse, holding the bridle. Don't do anything else till I tell you."

Mr. Duke begins to read the names.

"Barbara Adams—Twinkles." Barbara walks over to the right, where Mr. Duke has pointed.

"Melissa Babcock—Cinnamon." Now Barbara's horse, a chestnut brown mare, is being brought out to her. Barbara takes the reins from Greta as Melissa waits for her horse.

"Clara Chu—Starlight."

"Heidi Erickson—Flame."

"Felice Feinstein—Echo."

As Margaret waits, she realizes to her horror that the names are being called alphabetically. *What if there is no horse left for her?*

But when Mr. Duke reaches *Z*, there is still a horse, one horse, left.

"Margaret Ziegler." He pauses. "Hmmm," he says, "I guess it'll have to be Oleo."

Oleo! What kind of name is *that* for a horse?

Margaret stands at the end of the line of girls, each girl holding her horse.

And she sees Greta pulling on the bridle of a horse who does not want to come.

This horse is white, with big, ugly, brown blotches and a short, ugly mane that sticks straight up like the bristles on a toothbrush. This horse is big and fat— much fatter than any other horse Greta has brought out. Now Margaret knows why this horse, who still doesn't move, is named Oleo.

Greta slaps Oleo on the rump, and finally he moves. She brings him to Margaret. Margaret reaches up and takes him by the bridle. He is certainly big and fat. He is fatter than any horse Margaret has ever even seen a picture of. He is so fat it is scary.

Still Margaret holds the bridle.

Oleo looks down at Margaret. He shows his teeth. He pushes his ears back. He rolls his eyes in disgust.

Now Mr. Duke is coming.

"All right, girls," says Mr. Duke. "First we are going to talk about mounting and dismounting."

At that moment, something awful happens.

Oleo steps on Margaret's foot.

The doctor says that none of Margaret's toes are broken, but they are very badly bruised. He says she shouldn't bear down on that foot for a few days. He advises ice packs.

Margaret hobbles out to the car.

"Here, do you want me to help you?" asks her mother.

"No," says Margaret.

In the car, Margaret's mother says, "Honey, I'm *so* sorry. I know how much you were looking forward to this."

Margaret doesn't say anything. She just looks out the window.

When they get home, Margaret says, "I don't think I want to go back to Country Life Riding Day Camp anymore."

That night, Margaret sits in the big chair in the living room, her foot wrapped up in plastic bags of ice. A blue towel is wrapped around the plastic bags. Her mother is in the kitchen making lemon meringue pie— Margaret's favorite—for dessert, but Margaret doesn't care. Everything is awful.

The front door slams. In comes Rodney, tossing his softball. He looks at her.

"What happened to you?"

Margaret says, "A horse named Oleo stepped on my foot." Then she looks away from Rodney, and big tears begin to roll down her cheeks.

"Hey, great!" says Rodney, kneeling down next to her.

"What do you mean, great?" says Margaret. "Can't you just shut up and leave me alone for once?"

"No, really, I mean it," says Rodney. "It's great! It's your first sports injury. Remember when I got shin splints running track? Remember when I sprained my pitching arm?"

"Well," says Margaret, snuffling, "it may be my first sports injury, but it's also my last. I am never going near another horse for as long as I live. I'm going to take Arts and Crafts at the Youth Center if they still have room. Mom already said I could."

"Well, you *can,* Mags," says Rodney. "But it would be very, very wimpy. You ought to try again. You don't think anybody's perfect the first time they try something, do you?"

Margaret doesn't say anything. Her only consolation is that she has never told her family about Midnight.

"Look," says Rodney, "in all those horse books, didn't it ever say something about how, when you're thrown from a horse, you have to get right back on so you won't get scared?"

"Sure," says Margaret. "But I didn't even get on."

"All the more reason," says Rodney, and he stands up and goes upstairs to change, tossing his softball.

At dinner, Margaret's mother tells Margaret's father
what has happened. Margaret's father is very
sympathetic. Margaret's mother tells Margaret's father
that Margaret has decided to switch to Arts and Crafts
at the Youth Center if there's still room. "Of course.
Perfectly understandable," says Margaret's father.

"Well, wait," says Margaret. She hasn't said much during dinner. Everyone turns and looks at her. "I've been thinking about it," she says, "and I think maybe I would like to try Country Life Riding Day Camp again. Just try it. When my foot is better. Maybe not every day, but a couple of times a week. And go to Arts and Crafts at the Youth Center the other days, if I could."

"That's my girl," says her mother, smiling.

"Smart thinking," says her father, nodding. "That's a more well-rounded approach, anyway."

"Way to go, Margaret!" says Rodney. "Aw-right!"

Margaret has two pieces of lemon meringue pie for dessert.

F   3617
DRA   Dragonwagon, Cres-
                  cent

             Margaret Ziegler
             is horse-crazy

F   3617
DRA